In Level 0, **Step 8** builds o
previous steps and introd
their letters:

ar   or   ur   ov

Special features:

Repetition of sounds
in different words

Short sentences with
simple language

The sun sets as the cows
finish the song.

Barn Owl is not sad at all.

How are you
now, Barn Owl?

I am better!
Hoot!

Phonically
decodable
text builds
reading
confidence

14

15

Story Words

Can you match these words
to the pictures?

park

cows

owl

farm

shark

Tricky Words

These tricky words are in the story
you have just read. They cannot
be sounded out. Can you memorize
them and read them super fast?

he

all

the

into

you

17

Summary page to
reinforce learning

Practice of words that
cannot be sounded out

Educational consultant: Geraldine Taylor

Phonics and Book Banding Consultant: Kate Ruttle

LADYBIRD BOOKS

UK | USA | Canada | Ireland | Australia
India | New Zealand | South Africa

Ladybird Books is part of the Penguin Random House group of companies
whose addresses can be found at global.penguinrandomhouse.com.

www.penguin.co.uk www.puffin.co.uk www.ladybird.co.uk

Penguin
Random House
UK

First edition published 2020
001

Copyright © Ladybird Books Ltd, 2020

Printed in China

A CIP catalogue record for this book is available from the British Library

ISBN: 978-0-241-40511-6

All correspondence to
Ladybird Books
Penguin Random House Children's
80 Strand, London WC2R 0RL

Barn Owl

Written by Claire Smith
Illustrated by Dean Gray

Barn Owl is ill.
He can not hoot.

In the park, he sees
Lars the Shark.

A-tish-oo!

Good
morning,
Barn Owl.

Lars has a hat for Barn Owl!

You are
a good pal,
Lars!

Barn Owl is less sad now.
On the farm, he sees
the cows.

The cows turn and chat.
How can Barn Owl get
better?

A-tish-oo!

Barn Owl gets into bed.
The cows sing.

Moo! Moo!

The duck joins in, too!
Barn Owl naps.

The sun sets as the cows
finish the song.

How are you
now, Barn Owl?

Barn Owl is not sad at all.

I am better! Hoot!

Story Words

Can you match these words
to the pictures?

park

cows

owl

farm

shark

Tricky Words

These tricky words are in the story you have just read. They cannot be sounded out. Can you memorize them and read them super fast?

he

all

the

into

you

Look in the Box!

Written by Claire Smith
Illustrated by Dean Gray

Barn Owl looks in the box.
He sees a cap, boots and
a big fork.

Barn Owl is a farmer!

I can dig the soil.
I can pull up the
turnips.

Barn Owl looks in the box.
He sees red shorts and a top.

Barn Owl is a surfer!

Look at my shorts!

Barn Owl sees a cook's hat
and a jar of jam in the box.

Owl Chick sees the box.

Owl Chick looks in the box.

I can be a queen . . .

. . . or a singer!

27

Barn Owl is back.

Look at all this mess!

Barn Owl looks in the box.
He sees a monster!

Story Words

Can you match these words
to the pictures?

fork

soil

surfer

jar

singer

monster